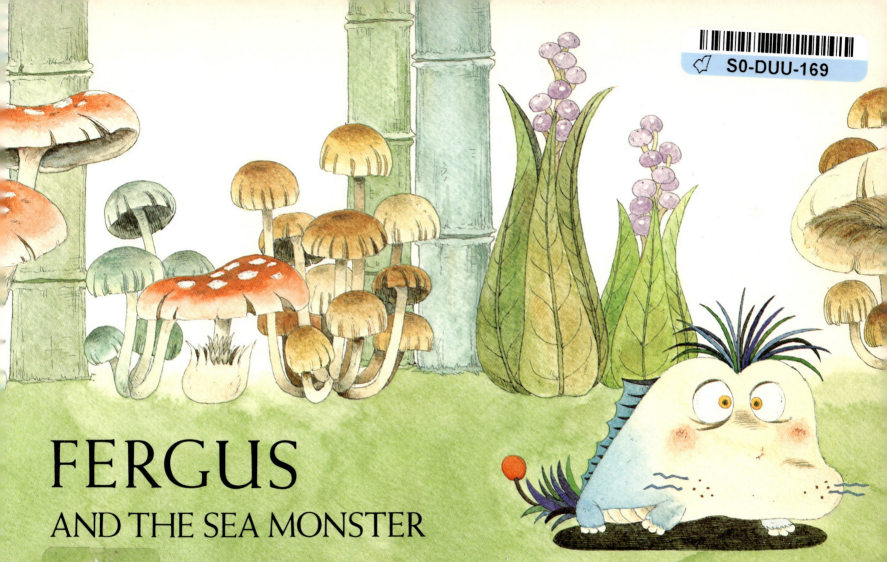

FERGUS
AND THE SEA MONSTER

by Yasuko Kimura

© 1976 Shiko-Sha. All Rights Reserved. Printed in Japan.
First distribution in the United States of America by McGraw-Hill, Inc., 1977.
Cataloging in Publication Data appears on last page.

McGraw-Hill Book Company   New York   St. Louis   San Francisco

Early one morning, Fergus the puppy was munching hungrily on some fish when a funny little animal with a blue coat and big eyes toddled up to him.

"Where did you come from, Big Eyes?" Fergus asked, and without thinking, tossed the little animal a fish. What a mistake that was!

Big Eyes ate the fish right up, and from that moment on, followed Fergus everywhere he went. Fergus climbed up to give his friend Milton some fish, and Big Eyes scrambled over the rocks right after him. And everywhere he went he ate—plants, trees, fish—anything he could get his teeth into.

"Where did you find him, Fergus?" Tony Turtle asked.

"I didn't find him," Fergus answered. "He found me."

"You never know what he will eat next!" Tony said.

"I just remembered something I have to do. So long, Fergus."

All of Fergus's other friends remembered something they had to do, too. Only Lori the ladybug stayed with Fergus. She never wanted to miss anything.

Fergus thought Big Eyes looked sleepy.
"You go home now," Fergus told him.
"Sleep in your own place,
 wherever that is."

Big Eyes didn't say a word.
He brought a flower to Fergus
and cuddled up close to him.

"What a pest!" Fergus cried. He ran away and hid in some logs. Big Eyes ran right after him. He ate his way through the logs until he caught up with Fergus.

After that, Fergus tried other ways to send him away.

But Big Eyes brought Fergus a lovely dragonfly and tried to cuddle up close to him again. That's when Fergus noticed something else about him.

"You're growing!" Fergus exclaimed. "No wonder! You never stop eating. Big eyes! Big stomach! You're a **monster!** Go away and let me alone. I'm going fishing," said Fergus.
"You will scare the fish away."

Fergus had caught only three tiny fish when Big Eyes was back again.
He was pushing the biggest fish Fergus had ever seen.

They had just started to eat, when Fergus heard a noise. He turned around and there was an ugly, giant rat reaching out to grab the fish.

Fergus barked in fright and ran.

But Big Eyes jumped on the giant rat.

He gave him such a chewing-over the rat scuttled away, dragging his tail behind him.

Later that day, Fergus said, "You know—you are quite a fighter, Big Eyes. How would you like to be friends?"

From then on, the two new friends had lots of fun together. They watched the sun rise and set. They raced snails and played other games.

The only trouble for Fergus was that Big Eyes still liked to cuddle close to him, and still ate everything he could and kept growing bigger and bigger.

One night they were sleeping in Fergus's cave when Fergus woke up to discover two great, big eyes staring in at him.

Fergus stared back and saw a strange animal with a blue coat and big eyes. It looked just like Big Eyes but it was at least four times as big as Fergus's friend! "So that's where you are, son," the strange animal said to Big Eyes. "I never thought of looking on land for you until tonight. My how you've grown!"

"Don't you know the sea is where you belong? Come along now. I want to get back home to the deep, cool sea before that hot sun rises much higher in the sky." Fergus wanted his friend to stay. Big Eyes wanted to stay, too, but his Mother just hurried him along.

Fergus felt very sad when his friend was gone. He cuddled up to the top of a rock as close to the sea as he could get.

The dragonfly and Lori the ladybug tried to cheer him.

"Stop moping, Fergus," Lori said. "Milton's having a party. Tony and all the others are going. They want you to come, too."

But Fergus just shook his head.
Suddenly Lori cried: "Look, Fergus. Look in back of you, over there!"

"It's Big Eyes, bigger than ever. Look what he's got for you now, Fergus. It's a whale! See, he **didn't** forget you."

Library of Congress Cataloging in Publication Data

Kimura, Yasuko. Fergus and the sea monster.
Summary: Fergus doesn't know what to do with
the funny blue monster who is growing bigger and
bigger and following him everywhere.
[1. Dogs—Fiction. 2. Monsters—Fiction] I. Title.
PZ7.K56495Ff [E] 77-7089
ISBN 0-07-034558-9   ISBN 0-07-034559-7 lib. bdg.